This Little Seed

Heather Hammonds
Photographs by Bill Thomas

NELSON

★

™

THOMSON LEARNING

Australia · Canada · Mexico · Singapore · Spain · United Kingdom · United States

Can you see
this little seed?

To make it grow,

what will you need?

Water and soil,

and sunshine, too.

Can this seed grow
as tall as you?

8

This seed will sprout,
just watch it go.

This little seed
will grow and grow!

This seed will grow, and you will see,

This little seed

is now a tree.